Madame Delphine

MW00901677

1

Madame Delphine

by George Washington Cable

CHAPTER I.

AN OLD HOUSE.

A few steps from the St. Charles Hotel, in New Orleans, brings you to and across Canal street, the central avenue of the city, and to that corner where the flower-women sit at the inner and outer edges of the arcaded sidewalk, and make the air sweet with their fragrant merchandise. The crowd—and if it is near the time of the carnival it will be great—will follow Canal street.

But you turn, instead, into the quiet, narrow way which a lover of Creole antiquity, in fondness for a romantic past, is still prone to call the Rue Royale. You will pass a few restaurants, a few auction rooms, a few furniture warehouses, and will hardly realize that you have left behind you the activity and clatter of a city of merchants before you find yourself in a region of architectural decrepitude, where an ancient and foreign-seeming domestic life, in second stories, overhangs the ruins of a former commercial prosperity, and upon everything has settled down a long Sabbath of decay. The vehicles in the street are few in number, and are merely passing through; the stores are shrunken into shops; you see here and there, like a patch of bright mould, the stall of that significant fungus, the Chinaman. Many great doors are shut and clamped and grown gray with cobweb; many street windows are nailed up; half the balconies are begrimed and rust-eaten, and many of the humid arches and alleys which characterize the older Franco-Spanish piles of stuccoed brick betray a squalor almost oriental.

Yet beauty lingers here. To say nothing of the picturesque, sometimes you get sight of comfort, sometimes of opulence, through the unlatched wicket in some *porte-cochère*—red-painted brick pavement, foliage of dark palm or pale banana, marble or granite masonry and blooming parterres; or through a chink between some pair of heavy batten window-shutters, opened with an almost reptile wariness, your eye gets a glimpse of lace and brocade upholstery, silver and bronze, and much similar rich antiquity.

The faces of the inmates are in keeping; of the passengers in the street a sad proportion are dingy and shabby; but just when these are putting you off your guard, there will pass you a woman—more likely two or three—of patrician beauty.

Now, if you will go far enough down this old street, you will see, as you approach its intersection with——. Names in that region elude one like ghosts.

However, as you begin to find the way a trifle more open, you will not fail to notice on the right-hand side, about midway of the square, a small, low, brick house of a story and a half, set out upon the sidewalk, as weather-beaten and mute as an aged beggar fallen asleep. Its corrugated roof of dull red tiles, sloping down toward you with an inward curve, is overgrown with weeds, and in the fall of the year is gay with the yellow plumes of the golden-rod. You can almost touch with your cane the low edge of the broad, overhanging eaves. The batten shutters at door and window, with hinges like those of a postern, are shut with a grip that makes one's knuckles and nails feel lacerated. Save in the brick-work itself there is not a cranny. You would say the house has the lock-jaw. There are two doors, and to each a single chipped and battered marble step. Continuing on down the sidewalk, on a line with the house, is a garden masked from view by a high, close board-fence. You may see the tops of its fruit-trees—pomegranate, peach, banana, fig, pear, and particularly one large orange, close by the fence, that must be very old.

The residents over the narrow way, who live in a three-story house, originally of much pretension, but from whose front door hard times have removed almost all vestiges of paint, will tell you:

"Yass, de 'ouse is in'abit; 'tis live in."

And this is likely to be all the information you get—not that they would not tell, but they cannot grasp the idea that you wish to know—until, possibly, just as you are turning to depart, your informant, in a single word and with the most evident non-appreciation of its value, drops the simple key to the whole matter:

"Dey's quadroons."

He may then be aroused to mention the better appearance of the place in former years, when the houses of this region generally stood farther apart, and that garden comprised the whole square.

Here dwelt, sixty years ago and more, one Delphine Carraze; or, as she was commonly designated by the few who knew her, Madame Delphine. That she owned her home, and that it had been

a person of 1/4 black ancestry)

given her by the then deceased companion of her days of beauty, were facts so generally admitted as to be, even as far back as that sixty years ago, no longer a subject of gossip. She was never pointed out by the denizens of the quarter as a character, nor her house as a "feature." It would have passed all Creole powers of guessing to divine what you could find worthy of inquiry concerning a retired quadroon woman; and not the least puzzled of all would have been the timid and restive Madame Delphine herself.

CHAPTER II.
MADAME DELPHINE.

During the first quarter of the present century, the free quadroon caste of New Orleans was in its golden age. Earlier generations— sprung, upon the one hand, from the merry gallants of a French colonial military service which had grown gross by affiliation with Spanish-American frontier life, and, upon the other hand, from comely Ethiopians culled out of the less negroidal types of African live goods, and bought at the ship's side with vestiges of quills and cowries and copper wire still in their head-dresses,—these earlier generations, with scars of battle or private rencontre still on the fathers, and of servitude on the manumitted mothers, afforded a mere hint of the splendor that was to result from a survival of the fairest through seventy-five years devoted to the elimination of the black pigment and the cultivation of hyperian excellence and nymphean grace and beauty. Nor, if we turn to the present, is the evidence much stronger which is offered by the *gens de couleur* whom you may see in the quadroon quarter this afternoon, with "Ichabod" legible on their murky foreheads through a vain smearing of toilet powder, dragging their chairs down to the narrow gate-way of their close-fenced gardens, and staring shrinkingly at you as you pass, like a nest of yellow kittens.

But as the present century was in its second and third decades, the *quadroones* (for we must contrive a feminine spelling to define the strict limits of the caste as then established) came forth in splendor. Old travellers spare no terms to tell their praises, their faultlessness of feature, their perfection of form, their varied styles of beauty,—for there were even pure Caucasian blondes among

5

---

them,—their fascinating manners, their sparkling vivacity, their chaste and pretty wit, their grace in the dance, their modest propriety, their taste and elegance in dress. In the gentlest and most poetic sense they were indeed the sirens of this land, where it seemed "always afternoon"—a momentary triumph of an Arcadian over a Christian civilization, so beautiful and so seductive that it became the subject of special chapters by writers of the day more original than correct as social philosophers.

The balls that were got up for them by the male *sang-pur* were to that day what the carnival is to the present. Society balls given the same nights proved failures through the coincidence. The magnates of government,—municipal, state, federal,—those of the army, of the learned professions and of the clubs,—in short, the white male aristocracy in everything save the ecclesiastical desk,—were there. Tickets were high-priced to insure the exclusion of the vulgar. No distinguished stranger was allowed to miss them. They were beautiful! They were clad in silken extenuations from the throat to the feet, and wore, withal, a pathos in their charm that gave them a family likeness to innocence.

Madame Delphine, were you not a stranger, could have told you all about it; though hardly, I suppose, without tears.

But at the time of which we would speak (1821-22) her day of splendor was set, and her husband—let us call him so for her sake—was long dead. He was an American, and, if we take her word for it, a man of noble heart and extremely handsome; but this is knowledge which we can do without.

Even in those days the house was always shut, and Madame Delphine's chief occupation and end in life seemed to be to keep well locked up in-doors. She was an excellent person, the neighbors said,—a very worthy person; and they were, may be, nearer correct than they knew. They rarely saw her save when she went to or returned from church; a small, rather tired-looking, dark quadroone of very good features and a gentle thoughtfulness of expression which it would take long to describe: call it a widow's look.

In speaking of Madame Delphine's house, mention should have been made of a gate in the fence on the Royal-street sidewalk. It is gone now, and was out of use then, being fastened once for all by an iron staple clasping the cross-bar and driven into the post.

6

Which leads us to speak of another person.

CHAPTER III.
CAPITAINE LEMAITRE.

He was one of those men that might be any age,—thirty, forty, forty-five; there was no telling from his face what was years and what was only weather. His countenance was of a grave and quiet, but also luminous, sort, which was instantly admired and ever afterward remembered, as was also the fineness of his hair and the blueness of his eyes. Those pronounced him youngest who scrutinized his face the closest. But waiving the discussion of age, he was odd, though not with the oddness that he who reared him had striven to produce.

He had not been brought up by mother or father. He had lost both in infancy, and had fallen to the care of a rugged old military grandpa of the colonial school, whose unceasing endeavor had been to make "his boy" as savage and ferocious a holder of unimpeachable social rank as it became a pure-blooded French Creole to be who could trace his pedigree back to the god Mars.   *solemn oath*

"Remember, my boy," was the adjuration received by him as regularly as his waking cup of black coffee, "that none of your family line ever kept the laws of any government or creed." And if it was well that he should bear this in mind, it was well to reiterate it persistently, for, from the nurse's arms, the boy wore a look, not of docility so much as of gentle, *judicial* benevolence. The domestics of the old man's house used to shed tears of laughter to see that look on the face of a babe. His rude guardian addressed himself to the modification of this facial expression; it had not enough of majesty in it, for instance, or of large dare-deviltry; but with care these could be made to come.

And, true enough, at twenty-one (in Ursin Lemaitre), the labors of his grandfather were an apparent success. He was not rugged, nor was he loud-spoken, as his venerable trainer would have liked to present him to society; but he was as serenely terrible as a well-aimed rifle, and the old man looked upon his results with pride. He had cultivated him up to that pitch where he scorned to practice any vice, or any virtue, that did not include the principle of self-assertion. A few touches only were wanting here and there to achieve perfection, when suddenly the old man died. Yet it was his proud satisfaction, before he finally lay down, to see Ursin a favored companion and the peer, both in courtesy and pride, of those polished gentlemen famous in history, the brothers Lafitte.

The two Lafittes were, at the time young Lemaitre reached his majority (say 1808 or 1812), only merchant blacksmiths, so to speak, a term intended to convey the idea of blacksmiths who never soiled their hands, who were men of capital, stood a little higher than the clergy, and moved in society among its autocrats. But they were full of possibilities, men of action, and men, too, of thought, with already a pronounced disbelief in the custom-house. In these days of big carnivals they would have been patented as the dukes of Little Manchac and Barataria.

Young Ursin Lemaitre (in full the name was Lemaitre-Vignevielle) had not only the hearty friendship of these good people, but also a natural turn for accounts; and as his two friends were looking about them with an enterprising eye, it easily resulted that he presently connected himself with the blacksmithing profession. Not exactly at the forge in the Lafittes' famous smithy, among the African Samsons, who, with their shining black bodies bared to the waist, made the Rue St. Pierre ring with the stroke of their hammers; but as a—there was no occasion to mince the word in those days—smuggler.

Smuggler—patriot—where was the difference? Beyond the ken of a community to which the enforcement of the revenue laws had long been merely so much out of every man's pocket and dish, into the all-devouring treasury of Spain. At this date they had come under a kinder yoke, and to a treasury that at least echoed when the customs were dropped into it; but the change was still new. What could a man be more than Capitaine Lemaitre was—the soul of honor, the pink of courtesy, with the courage of the lion, and the magnanimity of the elephant; frank—the very exchequer of truth! Nay, go higher still: his paper was good in Toulouse street. To the gossips in the gaming-clubs he was the culminating proof that smuggling was one of the sublimer virtues.

Years went by. Events transpired which have their place in history. Under a government which the community by and by saw was conducted in their interest, smuggling began to lose its respectability and to grow disreputable, hazardous, and debased. In certain onslaughts made upon them by officers of the law, some of the smugglers became murderers. The business became unprofitable for a time until the enterprising Lafittes—thinkers—bethought them of a corrective—"privateering."

Thereupon the United States Government set a price upon their heads. Later yet it became known that these outlawed pirates had been offered money and rank by Great Britain if they would join her standard, then hovering about the water-approaches to their native city, and that they had spurned the bribe; wherefore their heads were ruled out of the market, and, meeting and treating with Andrew Jackson, they were received as lovers of their country, and as compatriots fought in the battle of New Orleans at the head of their fearless men, and—here tradition takes up the tale—were never seen afterward.

Capitaine Lemaitre was not among the killed or wounded, but he was among the missing.

CHAPTER IV.
THREE FRIENDS.

The roundest and happiest-looking priest in the city of New Orleans was a little man fondly known among his people as Père Jerome. He was a Creole and a member of one of the city's leading families. His dwelling was a little frame cottage, standing on high pillars just inside a tall, close fence, and reached by a narrow outdoor stair from the green batten gate. It was well surrounded by crape myrtles, and communicated behind by a descending stair and a plank-walk with the rear entrance of the chapel over whose worshippers he daily spread his hands in benediction. The name of the street—ah! there is where light is wanting. Save the Cathedral and the Ursulines, there is very little of record concerning churches at that time, though they were springing up here and there. All there is certainty of is that Père Jerome's frame chapel was some little new-born "down-town" thing, that may have survived the passage of years, or may have escaped "Paxton's Directory" "so as by fire." His parlor was dingy and carpetless; one could smell distinctly there the vow of poverty. His bedchamber was bare and clean, and the bed in it narrow and hard; but between the two was a dining-room that would tempt a laugh to the lips of any who looked in. The table was small, but stout, and all the furniture of the room substantial, made of fine wood, and carved just enough to give the notion of wrinkling pleasantry. His mother's and sister's doing, Père Jerome would explain; they would not permit this apartment—or department—to suffer. Therein, as well as in the parlor, there was odor, but of a more epicurean sort, that explained interestingly the Père Jerome's rotundity and rosy smile.

In this room, and about this miniature round table, used sometimes to sit with Père Jerome two friends to whom he was deeply attached—one, Evariste Varrillat, a playmate from early childhood, now his brother-in-law; the other, Jean Thompson, a companion from youngest manhood, and both, like the little priest himself, the regretful rememberers of a fourth comrade who was a comrade no more. Like Père Jerome, they had come, through years, to the thick of life's conflicts,—the priest's brother-in-law a physician, the other an attorney, and brother-in-law to the lonely wanderer,—yet they loved to huddle around this small board, and be boys again in heart while men in mind. Neither one nor another was leader. In earlier days they had always yielded to him who no longer met with them a certain chieftainship, and they still thought of him and talked of him, and, in their conjectures, groped after him, as one of whom they continued to expect greater things than of themselves.

They sat one day drawn thus close together, sipping and theorizing, speculating upon the nature of things in an easy, bold, sophomoric way, the conversation for the most part being in French, the native tongue of the doctor and priest, and spoken with facility by Jean Thompson the lawyer, who was half Américain; but running sometimes into English and sometimes into mild laughter. Mention had been made of the absentee.

Père Jerome advanced an idea something like this:

"It is impossible for any finite mind to fix the degree of criminality of any human act or of any human life. The Infinite One alone can know how much of our sin is chargeable to us, and how much to our brothers or our fathers. We all participate in one another's sins. There is a community of responsibility attaching to every misdeed. No human since Adam—nay, nor Adam himself—ever sinned entirely to himself. And so I never am called upon to contemplate a crime or a criminal but I feel my conscience pointing at me as one of the accessories."

"In a word," said Evariste Varrillat, the physician, "you think we are partly to blame for the omission of many of your Paternosters, eh?"

Father Jerome smiled.

"No; a man cannot plead so in his own defense; our first father tried that, but the plea was not allowed. But, now, there is our absent friend. I tell you truly this whole community ought to be recognized as partners in his moral errors. Among another people, reared under wiser care and with better companions, how different might he not have been! How can *we* speak of him as a law-breaker who might have saved him from that name?" Here the speaker turned to Jean Thompson, and changed his speech to English. "A lady sez to me to-day: 'Père Jerome, 'ow dat is a dreadfool dat 'e gone at de coas' of Cuba to be one corsair! Aint it?' 'Ah, Madame,' I sez, "tis a terrible! I'ope de good God will fo'give me an' you fo' dat!'"

Jean Thompson answered quickly:

"You should not have let her say that."

"*Mais*, fo' w'y?"

"Why, because, if you are partly responsible, you ought so much the more to do what you can to shield his reputation. You should have said,"—the attorney changed to French,—"'He is no pirate; he has merely taken out letters of marque and reprisal under the flag of the republic of Carthagena!'"

"*Ah, bah!*" exclaimed Doctor Varrillat, and both he and his brother-in-law, the priest, laughed.

"Why not?" demanded Thompson.

"Oh!" said the physician, with a shrug, "say id thad way iv you wand."

Then, suddenly becoming serious, he was about to add something else, when Père Jerome spoke.

"I will tell you what I could have said. I could have said: 'Madame, yes; 'tis a terrible fo' him. He stum'le in de dark; but dat good God will mek it a *mo' terrible* fo' dat man, oohever he is, w'at put 'at light out!'"

"But how do you know he is a pirate?" demanded Thompson, aggressively.

"How do we know?" said the little priest, returning to French. "Ah! there is no other explanation of the ninety-and-nine stories that come to us, from every port where ships arrive from the north coast of Cuba, of a commander of pirates there who is a marvel of courtesy and gentility——"*

"And whose name is Lafitte," said the obstinate attorney.

"And who, nevertheless, is not Lafitte," insisted Père Jerome.

"Daz troo, Jean," said Doctor Varrillat. "We hall know daz troo."

Père Jerome leaned forward over the board and spoke, with an air of secrecy, in French.

"You have heard of the ship which came into port here last Monday. You have heard that she was boarded by pirates, and that the captain of the ship himself drove them off."

"An incredible story," said Thompson.

"But not so incredible as the truth. I have it from a passenger. There was on the ship a young girl who was very beautiful. She came on deck, where the corsair stood, about to issue his orders, and, more beautiful than ever in the desperation of the moment, confronted him with a small missal spread open, and, her finger on the Apostles' Creed, commanded him to read. He read it, uncovering his head as he read, then stood gazing on her face, which did not quail; and then, with a low bow, said: 'Give me this book and I will do your bidding.' She gave him the book and bade him leave the ship, and he left it unmolested."

Père Jerome looked from the physician to the attorney and back again, once or twice, with his dimpled smile.

"But he speaks English, they say," said Jean Thompson.

"He has, no doubt, learned it since he left us," said the priest.

"But this ship-master, too, says his men called him Lafitte."

"Lafitte? No. Do you not see? It is your brother-in-law, Jean Thompson! It is your wife's brother! Not Lafitte, but" (softly) "Lemaitre! Lemaitre! Capitaine Ursin Lemaitre!"

The two guests looked at each other with a growing drollery on either face, and presently broke into a laugh.

"Ah!" said the doctor, as the three rose up, "you juz kip dad cog-an'-bull fo' yo' negs summon."

Père Jerome's eyes lighted up—

"I goin' to do it!"

12

"I tell you," said Evariste, turning upon him with sudden gravity, "iv dad is troo, I tell you w'ad is sure-sure! Ursin Lemaitre din kyare nut'n fo' doze creed; *he fall in love!*"

Then, with a smile, turning to Jean Thompson, and back again to Père Jerome:

"But anny'ow you tell it in dad summon dad 'e kyare fo' dad creed."

Père Jerome sat up late that night, writing a letter. The remarkable effects upon a certain mind, effects which we shall presently find him attributing solely to the influences of surrounding nature, may find for some a more sufficient explanation in the fact that this letter was but one of a series, and that in the rover of doubted identity and incredible eccentricity Père Jerome had a regular correspondent.

CHAPTER V.
THE CAP FITS.

About two months after the conversation just given, and therefore somewhere about the Christmas holidays of the year 1821, Père Jerome delighted the congregation of his little chapel with the announcement that he had appointed to preach a sermon in French on the following Sabbath—not there, but in the cathedral.

He was much beloved. Notwithstanding that among the clergy there were two or three who shook their heads and raised their eyebrows, and said he would be at least as orthodox if he did not make quite so much of the Bible and quite so little of the dogmas, yet "the common people heard him gladly." When told, one day, of the unfavorable whispers, he smiled a little and answered his informant,—whom he knew to be one of the whisperers himself,— laying a hand kindly upon his shoulder:

"Father Murphy,"—or whatever the name was,—"your words comfort me."

"How is that?"

"Because—'*Væ quum benedixerint mihi homines!*'"*

The appointed morning, when it came, was one of those exquisite days in which there is such a universal harmony, that worship rises from the heart like a spring.

"Truly," said Père Jerome to the companion who was to assist him in the mass, "this is a Sabbath day which we do not have to make holy, but only to *keep* so."

May be it was one of the secrets of Père Jerome's success as a preacher, that he took more thought as to how he should feel, than as to what he should say.

The cathedral of those days was called a very plain old pile, boasting neither beauty nor riches; but to Père Jerome it was very lovely; and before its homely altar, not homely to him, in the performance of those solemn offices, symbols of heaven's mightiest truths, in the hearing of the organ's harmonies, and the yet more eloquent interunion of human voices in the choir, in overlooking the worshipping throng which knelt under the soft, chromatic lights, and in breathing the sacrificial odors of the chancel, he found a deep and solemn joy; and yet I guess the finest thought of his soul the while was one that came thrice and again:

"Be not deceived, Père Jerome, because saintliness of feeling is easy here; you are the same priest who overslept this morning, and overate yesterday, and will, in some way, easily go wrong to-morrow and the day after."

He took it with him when—the *Veni Creator* sung—he went into the pulpit. Of the sermon he preached, tradition has preserved for us only a few brief sayings, but they are strong and sweet.

"My friends," he said,—this was near the beginning,—"the angry words of God's book are very merciful—they are meant to drive us home; but the tender words, my friends, they are sometimes terrible! Notice these, the tenderest words of the tenderest prayer that ever came from the lips of a blessed martyr—the dying words of the holy Saint Stephen, 'Lord, lay not this sin to their charge.' Is there nothing dreadful in that? Read it thus: 'Lord, lay not this sin to *their* charge.' Not to the charge of them who stoned him? To whose charge then? Go ask the holy Saint Paul. Three years afterward, praying in the temple at Jerusalem, he answered that question: 'I stood by and consented.' He answered for himself only; but the Day must come when all that wicked council that sent Saint Stephen away to be stoned, and all that city of Jerusalem, must hold up the hand and say: 'We, also, Lord—we stood by.' Ah! friends, under the simpler meaning of that dying saint's prayer for

14

the pardon of his murderers is hidden the terrible truth that we all have a share in one another's sins."

Thus Père Jerome touched his key-note. All that time has spared us beside may be given in a few sentences.

"Ah!" he cried once, "if it were merely my own sins that I had to answer for, I might hold up my head before the rest of mankind; but no, no, my friends—we cannot look each other in the face, for each has helped the other to sin. Oh, where is there any room, in this world of common disgrace, for pride? Even if we had no common hope, a common despair ought to bind us together and forever silence the voice of scorn!"

no room for pride

And again, this:

"Even in the promise to Noë, not again to destroy the race with a flood, there is a whisper of solemn warning. The moral account of the antediluvians was closed off and the balance brought down in the year of the deluge; but the account of those who come after runs on and on, and the blessed bow of promise itself warns us that God will not stop it till the Judgment Day! O God, I thank thee that that day must come at last, when thou wilt destroy the world, and stop the interest on my account!"

It was about at this point that Père Jerome noticed, more particularly than he had done before, sitting among the worshippers near him, a small, sad-faced woman, of pleasing features, but dark and faded, who gave him profound attention. With her was another in better dress, seemingly a girl still in her teens, though her face and neck were scrupulously concealed by a heavy veil, and her hands, which were small, by gloves.

"Quadroones," thought he, with a stir of deep pity.

Once, as he uttered some stirring word, he saw the mother and daughter (if such they were), while they still bent their gaze upon him, clasp each other's hand fervently in the daughter's lap. It was at these words:

"My friends, there are thousands of people in this city of New Orleans to whom society gives the ten commandments of God with all the *nots* rubbed out! Ah! good gentlemen! if God sends the poor weakling to purgatory for leaving the right path, where ought some of you to go who strew it with thorns and briers!"

The movement of the pair was only seen because he watched for it. He glanced that way again as he said:

"O God, be very gentle with those children who would be nearer heaven this day had they never had a father and mother, but had got their religious training from such a sky and earth as we have in Louisiana this holy morning! Ah! my friends, nature is a big-print catechism!"

The mother and daughter leaned a little farther forward, and exchanged the same spasmodic hand-pressure as before. The mother's eyes were full of tears.

"I once knew a man," continued the little priest, glancing to a side aisle where he had noticed Evariste and Jean sitting against each other, "who was carefully taught, from infancy to manhood, this single only principle of life: defiance. Not justice, not righteousness, not even gain; but defiance: defiance to God, defiance to man, defiance to nature, defiance to reason; defiance and defiance and defiance."

defiance

"He is going to tell it!" murmured Evariste to Jean.

"This man," continued Père Jerome, "became a smuggler and at last a pirate in the Gulf of Mexico. Lord, lay not that sin to his charge alone! But a strange thing followed. Being in command of men of a sort that to control required to be kept at the austerest distance, he now found himself separated from the human world and thrown into the solemn companionship with the sea, with the air, with the storm, the calm, the heavens by day, the heavens by night. My friends, that was the first time in his life that he ever found himself in really good company.

"Now, this man had a great aptness for accounts. He had kept them—had rendered them. There was beauty, to him, in a correct, balanced, and closed account. An account unsatisfied was a deformity. The result is plain. That man, looking out night after night upon the grand and holy spectacle of the starry deep above and the watery deep below, was sure to find himself, sooner or later, mastered by the conviction that the great Author of this majestic creation keeps account of it; and one night there came to him, like a spirit walking on the sea, the awful, silent question: 'My account with God—how does it stand?' Ah! friends, that is a question which the book of nature does not answer.

"Did I say the book of nature is a catechism? Yes. But, after it answers the first question with 'God,' nothing but questions follow; and so, one day, this man gave a ship full of merchandise for one

16

book of nature

little book which answered those questions. God help him to understand it! and God help you, monsieur and you, madame, sitting here in your *smuggled clothes*, to beat upon the breast with me and cry, 'I, too, Lord—I, too, stood by and consented.'"

Père Jerome had not intended these for his closing words; but just there, straight away before his sight and almost at the farthest door, a man rose slowly from his seat and regarded him steadily with a kind, bronzed, sedate face, and the sermon, as if by a sign of command, was ended. While the *Credo* was being chanted he was still there; but when, a moment after its close, the eye of Père Jerome returned in that direction, his place was empty.

As the little priest, his labor done and his vestments changed, was turning into the Rue Royale and leaving the cathedral out of sight, he just had time to understand that two women were purposely allowing him to overtake them, when the one nearer him spoke in the Creole patois, saying, with some timid haste:

"Good-morning, Père—Père Jerome; Père Jerome, we thank the good God for that sermon."

"Then, so do I," said the little man. They were the same two that he had noticed when he was preaching. The younger one bowed silently; she was a beautiful figure, but the slight effort of Père Jerome's kind eyes to see through the veil was vain. He would presently have passed on, but the one who had spoken before said:

"I thought you lived in the Rue des Ursulines."

"Yes; I am going this way to see a sick person."

The woman looked up at him with an expression of mingled confidence and timidity.

"It must be a blessed thing to be so useful as to be needed by the good God," she said.

Père Jerome smiled:

"God does not need me to look after his sick; but he allows me to do it, just as you let your little boy in frocks carry in chips." He might have added that he loved to do it, quite as much.

It was plain the woman had somewhat to ask, and was trying to get courage to ask it.

"You have a little boy?" asked the priest.

"No, I have only my daughter;" she indicated the girl at her side. Then she began to say something else, stopped, and with much nervousness asked:

"Père Jerome, what was the name of that man?"

"His name?" said the priest. "You wish to know his name?"

"Yes, Monsieur" (or *Miché*, as she spoke it); "it was such a beautiful story." The speaker's companion looked another way.

"His name," said Father Jerome,—"some say one name and some another. Some think it was Jean Lafitte, the famous; you have heard of him? And do you go to my church, Madame——?"

"No, Miché; not in the past; but from this time, yes. My name"— she choked a little, and yet it evidently gave her pleasure to offer this mark of confidence—"is Madame Delphine—Delphine Carraze."

CHAPTER VI.
A CRY OF DISTRESS.

Père Jerome's smile and exclamation, as some days later he entered his parlor in response to the announcement of a visitor, were indicative of hearty greeting rather than surprise.

"Madame Delphine!"

Yet surprise could hardly have been altogether absent, for though another Sunday had not yet come around, the slim, smallish figure sitting in a corner, looking very much alone, and clad in dark attire, which seemed to have been washed a trifle too often, was Delphine Carraze on her second visit. And this, he was confident, was over and above an attendance in the confessional, where he was sure he had recognized her voice.

She rose bashfully and gave her hand, then looked to the floor, and began a faltering speech, with a swallowing motion in the throat, smiled weakly and commenced again, speaking, as before, in a gentle, low note, frequently lifting up and casting down her eyes, while shadows of anxiety and smiles of apology chased each other rapidly across her face. She was trying to ask his advice.

"Sit down," said he; and when they had taken seats he resumed, with downcast eyes:

"You know,—probably I should have said this in the confessional, but—

"No matter, Madame Delphine; I understand; you did not want an oracle, perhaps; you want a friend."

She lifted her eyes, shining with tears, and dropped them again.

"I"—she ceased. "I have done a"—she dropped her head and shook it despondingly—"a cruel thing." The tears rolled from her eyes as she turned away her face.

Père Jerome remained silent, and presently she turned again, with the evident intention of speaking at length.

"It began nineteen years ago—by"—her eyes, which she had lifted, fell lower than ever, her brow and neck were suffused with blushes, and she murmured—"I fell in love."

She said no more, and by and by Père Jerome replied:

"Well, Madame Delphine, to love is the right of every soul. I believe in love. If your love was pure and lawful I am sure your angel guardian smiled upon you; and if it was not, I cannot say you have nothing to answer for, and yet I think God may have said: 'She is a quadroone; all the rights of her womanhood trampled in the mire, sin made easy to her—almost compulsory,—charge it to account of whom it may concern.'"

"No, no!" said Madame Delphine, looking up quickly, "some of it might fall upon—" Her eyes fell, and she commenced biting her lips and nervously pinching little folds in her skirt. "He was good—as good as the law would let him be—better, indeed, for he left me property, which really the strict law does not allow. He loved our little daughter very much. He wrote to his mother and sisters, owning all his error and asking them to take the child and bring her up. I sent her to them when he died, which was soon after, and did not see my child for sixteen years. But we wrote to each other all the time, and she loved me. And then—at last—" Madame Delphine ceased speaking, but went on diligently with her agitated fingers, turning down foolish hems lengthwise of her lap.

"At last your mother-heart conquered," said Père Jerome.

She nodded.

"The sisters married, the mother died; I saw that even where she was she did not escape the reproach of her birth and blood, and when she asked me to let her come—." The speaker's brimming eyes rose an instant. "I know it was wicked, but—I said, come."

The tears dripped through her hands upon her dress.

"Was it she who was with you last Sunday?"

"Yes."

"And now you do not know what to do with her?"

"*Ah! c'est ça, oui!*—that is it."

19

"Does she look like you, Madame Delphine?"

"Oh, thank God, no! you would never believe she was my daughter; she is white and beautiful!"

"You thank God for that which is your main difficulty, Madame Delphine."

"Alas! yes."

Père Jerome laid his palms tightly across his knees with his arms bowed out, and fixed his eyes upon the ground, pondering.

"I suppose she is a sweet, good daughter?" said he, glancing at Madame Delphine without changing his attitude.

Her answer was to raise her eyes rapturously.

"Which gives us the dilemma in its fullest force," said the priest, speaking as if to the floor. "She has no more place than if she had dropped upon a strange planet." He suddenly looked up with a brightness which almost as quickly passed away, and then he looked down again. His happy thought was the cloister; but he instantly said to himself: "They cannot have overlooked that choice, except intentionally—which they have a right to do." He could do nothing but shake his head.

"And suppose you should suddenly die," he said; he wanted to get at once to the worst.

The woman made a quick gesture, and buried her head in her handkerchief, with the stifled cry:

"Oh, Olive, my daughter!"

"Well, Madame Delphine," said Père Jerome, more buoyantly, "one thing is sure: we *must* find a way out of this trouble."

"Ah!" she exclaimed, looking heavenward, "if it might be!"

"But it must be!" said the priest.

"But how shall it be?" asked the desponding woman.

"Ah!" said Père Jerome, with a shrug, "God knows."

"Yes," said the quadroone, with a quick sparkle in her gentle eye; "and I know, if God would tell anybody, He would tell you!"

The priest smiled and rose.

"Do you think so? Well, leave me to think of it. I will ask Him."

"And He will tell you!" she replied. "And He will bless you!" She rose and gave her hand. As she withdrew it she smiled. "I had such a strange dream," she said, backing toward the door.

"Yes?"

"Yes. I got my troubles all mixed up with your sermon. I dreamed I made that pirate the guardian of my daughter."

Père Jerome smiled also, and shrugged.

"To you, Madame Delphine, as you are placed, every white man in this country, on land or on water, is a pirate, and of all pirates, I think that one is, without doubt, the best."

"Without doubt," echoed Madame Delphine, wearily, still withdrawing backward. Père Jerome stepped forward and opened the door.

The shadow of some one approaching it from without fell upon the threshold, and a man entered, dressed in dark blue cottonade, lifting from his head a fine Panama hat, and from a broad, smooth brow, fair where the hat had covered it and dark below, gently stroking back his very soft, brown locks. Madame Delphine slightly started aside, while Père Jerome reached silently, but eagerly, forward, grasped a larger hand than his own, and motioned its owner to a seat. Madame Delphine's eyes ventured no higher than to discover that the shoes of the visitor were of white duck.

"Well, Père Jerome," she said, in a hurried under-tone, "I am just going to say Hail Marys all the time till you find that out for me!"

"Well, I hope that will be soon, Madame Carraze. Good-day, Madame Carraze."

And as she departed, the priest turned to the new-comer and extended both hands, saying, in the same familiar dialect in which he had been addressing the quadroone:

"Well-a-day, old playmate! After so many years!"

They sat down side by side, like husband and wife, the priest playing with the other's hand, and talked of times and seasons past, often mentioning Evariste and often Jean.

Madame Delphine stopped short half-way home and returned to Père Jerome's. His entry door was wide open and the parlor door ajar. She passed through the one and with downcast eyes was standing at the other, her hand lifted to knock, when the door was drawn open and the white duck shoes passed out. She saw, besides, this time the blue cottonade suit.

"Yes," the voice of Père Jerome was saying, as his face appeared in the door—"Ah! Madame—"

"I lef' my para*sol*," said Madame Delphine, in English.

There was this quiet evidence of a defiant spirit hidden somewhere down under her general timidity, that, against a fierce conventional prohibition, she wore a bonnet instead of the turban of her caste, and carried a parasol.

Père Jerome turned and brought it.

He made a motion in the direction in which the late visitor had disappeared.

"Madame Delphine, you saw dat man?"

"Not his face."

"You couldn' billieve me iv I tell you w'at dat man pur*pose* to do!"

"Is dad so, Père Jerome?"

"He's goin' to hopen a bank!"

"Ah!" said Madame Delphine, seeing she was expected to be astonished.

Père Jerome evidently longed to tell something that was best kept secret; he repressed the impulse, but his heart had to say something. He threw forward one hand and looking pleasantly at Madame Delphine, with his lips dropped apart, clenched his extended hand and thrusting it toward the ground, said in a solemn under-tone:

"He is God's own banker, Madame Delphine."

CHAPTER VII.
MICHÉ VIGNEVIELLE.

Madame Delphine sold one of the corner lots of her property. She had almost no revenue, and now and then a piece had to go. As a consequence of the sale, she had a few large bank-notes sewed up in her petticoat, and one day—may be a fortnight after her tearful interview with Père Jerome—she found it necessary to get one of these changed into small money. She was in the Rue Toulouse, looking from one side to the other for a bank which was not in that street at all, when she noticed a small sign hanging above a door, bearing the name "Vignevielle." She looked in. Père Jerome had told her (when she had gone to him to ask where she should apply for change) that if she could only wait a few days, there would be a new concern opened in Toulouse street,—it really seemed as if Vignevielle was the name, if she could judge; it looked to be, and it was, a private banker's,—"U. L. Vignevielle's," according to a larger inscription which met her eyes as she ventured in. Behind the counter, exchanging some last words with a busy-mannered man outside, who, in withdrawing, seemed bent on running over Madame Delphine, stood the man in blue cottonade, whom she had met in Père Jerome's door-way. Now, for the first time, she saw his face, its strong, grave, human kindness shining softly on each and every bronzed feature. The recognition was mutual. He took pains to speak first, saying, in a re-assuring tone, and in the language he had last heard her use:

"'Ow I kin serve you, Madame?"

"Iv you pliz, to mague dad bill change, Miché."

She pulled from her pocket a wad of dark cotton handkerchief, from which she began to untie the imprisoned note. Madame Delphine had an uncommonly sweet voice, and it seemed so to strike Monsieur Vignevielle. He spoke to her once or twice more, as he waited on her, each time in English, as though he enjoyed the humble melody of its tone, and presently, as she turned to go, he said:

"Madame Carraze!"

She started a little, but bethought herself instantly that he had heard her name in Père Jerome's parlor. The good father might even have said a few words about her after her first departure; he had such an overflowing heart.

"Madame Carraze," said Monsieur Vignevielle, "doze kine of note wad you 'an' me juz now is bein' contrefit. You muz tek kyah from doze kine of note. You see—" He drew from his cash-drawer a note resembling the one he had just changed for her, and proceeded to point out certain tests of genuineness. The counterfeit, he said, was so and so.

"Bud," she exclaimed, with much dismay, "dad was de manner of my bill! Id muz be—led me see dad bill wad I give you,—if you pliz, Miché."

Monsieur Vignevielle turned to engage in conversation with an employé and a new visitor, and gave no sign of hearing Madame Delphine's voice. She asked a second time, with like result, lingered timidly, and as he turned to give his attention to a third visitor, reiterated:

"Miché Vignevielle, I wizh you pliz led——"

"Madame Carraze," he said, turning so suddenly as to make the frightened little woman start, but extending his palm with a show of frankness, and assuming a look of benignant patience, "'ow I kin fine doze note now, mongs' all de rez? Iv you pliz nod to mague me doze troub'."

The dimmest shadow of a smile seemed only to give his words a more kindly authoritative import, and as he turned away again with a manner suggestive of finality, Madame Delphine found no choice but to depart. But she went away loving the ground beneath the feet of Monsieur U. L. Vignevielle.

"Oh, Père Jerome!" she exclaimed in the corrupt French of her caste, meeting the little father on the street a few days later, "you told the truth that day in your parlor. *Mo conné li à c't heure.* I know him now; he is just what you called him."

"Why do you not make him *your* banker, also, Madame Delphine?"

"I have done so this very day!" she replied, with more happiness in her eyes than Père Jerome had ever before seen there.

"Madame Delphine," he said, his own eyes sparkling, "make *him* your daughter's guardian; for myself, being a priest, it would not be best; but ask him; I believe he will not refuse you."

Madame Delphine's face grew still brighter as he spoke.

"It was in my mind," she said.

Yet to the timorous Madame Delphine many trifles became, one after another, an impediment to the making of this proposal, and many weeks elapsed before further delay was positively without excuse. But at length, one day in May, 1822, in a small private office behind Monsieur Vignevielle's banking-room,—he sitting beside a table, and she, more timid and demure than ever, having just taken a chair by the door,—she said, trying, with a little bashful laugh, to make the matter seem unimportant, and yet with some tremor of voice:

"Miché Vignevielle, I bin maguing my will." (Having commenced their acquaintance in English, they spoke nothing else.)

"'Tis a good idy," responded the banker.

"I kin mague you de troub' to kib dad will fo' me, Miché Vignevielle?"

"Yez."

She looked up with grateful re-assurance; but her eyes dropped again as she said:

"Miché Vignevielle——" Here she choked, and began her peculiar motion of laying folds in the skirt of her dress, with trembling fingers. She lifted her eyes, and as they met the look of deep and placid kindness that was in his face, some courage returned, and she said:

"Miché."

"Wad you wand?" asked he, gently.

"If it arrive to me to die——"

"Yez?"

Her words were scarcely audible:

"I wand you teg kyah my lill' girl."

"You 'ave one lill' gal, Madame Carraze?"

She nodded with her face down.

"An' you godd some mo' chillen?"

"No."

"I nevva know dad, Madame Carraze. She's a lill' small gal?"

Mothers forget their daughters' stature. Madame Delphine said: "Yez."

For a few moments neither spoke, and then Monsieur Vignevielle said:

"I will do dad."

"Lag she been you' h-own?" asked the mother, suffering from her own boldness.

"She's a good lill' chile, eh?"

"Miché, she's a lill' hangel!" exclaimed Madame Delphine, with a look of distress.

"Yez; I teg kyah 'v 'er, lag my h-own. I mague you dad promise."

"But——" There was something still in the way, Madame Delphine seemed to think.

The banker waited in silence.

"I suppose you will want to see my lill' girl?"

He smiled; for she looked at him as if she would implore him to decline.

"Oh, I tek you' word fo' hall dad, Madame Carraze. It mague no differend wad she loog lag; I don' wan' see 'er."

Madame Delphine's parting smile—she went very shortly—was gratitude beyond speech.

Monsieur Vignevielle returned to the seat he had left, and resumed a newspaper,—the *Louisiana Gazette* in all probability,—which he had laid down upon Madame Delphine's entrance. His eyes fell upon a paragraph which had previously escaped his notice. There they rested. Either he read it over and over unwearyingly, or he was lost in thought. Jean Thompson entered.

"Now," said Mr. Thompson, in a suppressed tone, bending a little across the table, and laying one palm upon a package of papers which lay in the other, "it is completed. You could retire from your business any day inside of six hours without loss to anybody." (Both here and elsewhere, let it be understood that where good English is given the words were spoken in good French.)

Monsieur Vignevielle raised his eyes and extended the newspaper to the attorney, who received it and read the paragraph. Its substance was that a certain vessel of the navy had returned from a cruise in the Gulf of Mexico and Straits of Florida, where she had done valuable service against the pirates—having, for instance, destroyed in one fortnight in January last twelve pirate vessels afloat, two on the stocks, and three establishments ashore.

"United States brig *Porpoise*," repeated Jean Thompson. "Do you know her?"

"We are acquainted," said Monsieur Vignevielle.

CHAPTER VIII.
SHE.

A quiet footstep, a grave new presence on financial sidewalks, a neat garb slightly out of date, a gently strong and kindly pensive face, a silent bow, a new sign in the Rue Toulouse, a lone figure with a cane, walking in meditation in the evening light under the willows of Canal Marigny, a long-darkened window re-lighted in the Rue Conti—these were all; a fall of dew would scarce have been more quiet than was the return of Ursin Lemaitre-Vignevielle to the precincts of his birth and early life.

But we hardly give the event its right name. It was Capitaine Lemaitre who had disappeared; it was Monsieur Vignevielle who had come back. The pleasures, the haunts, the companions, that had once held out their charms to the impetuous youth, offered no enticements to Madame Delphine's banker. There is this to be said even for the pride his grandfather had taught him, that it had always held him above low indulgences; and though he had dallied with kings, queens, and knaves through all the mazes of Faro, Rondeau, and Craps, he had done it loftily; but now he maintained a peaceful estrangement from all. Evariste and Jean, themselves, found him only by seeking.

"It is the right way," he said to Père Jerome, the day we saw him there. "Ursin Lemaitre is dead. I have buried him. He left a will. I am his executor."

"He is crazy," said his lawyer brother-in-law, impatiently.

"On the contr-y," replied the little priest, "'e 'as come ad hisse'f." Evariste spoke.

"Look at his face, Jean. Men with that kind of face are the last to go crazy."

"You have not proved that," replied Jean, with an attorney's obstinacy. "You should have heard him talk the other day about that newspaper paragraph. 'I have taken Ursin Lemaitre's head; I have it with me; I claim the reward, but I desire to commute it to citizenship.' He is crazy."

Of course Jean Thompson did not believe what he said; but he said it, and, in his vexation, repeated it, on the *banquettes* and at the clubs; and presently it took the shape of a sly rumor, that the returned rover was a trifle snarled in his top-hamper.

This whisper was helped into circulation by many trivial eccentricities of manner, and by the unaccountable oddness of some of his transactions in business.

"My dear sir!" cried his astounded lawyer, one day, "you are not running a charitable institution!"

"How do you know?" said Monsieur Vignevielle. There the conversation ceased.

"Why do you not found hospitals and asylums at once," asked the attorney, at another time, with a vexed laugh, "and get the credit of it?"

"And make the end worse than the beginning," said the banker, with a gentle smile, turning away to a desk of books.

"Bah!" muttered Jean Thompson.

Monsieur Vignevielle betrayed one very bad symptom. Wherever he went he seemed looking for somebody. It may have been perceptible only to those who were sufficiently interested in him to study his movements; but those who saw it once saw it always. He never passed an open door or gate but he glanced in; and often, where it stood but slightly ajar, you might see him give it a gentle push with his hand or cane. It was very singular.

He walked much alone after dark. The *guichinangoes* (garroters, we might say), at those times the city's particular terror by night, never crossed his path. He was one of those men for whom danger appears to stand aside.

One beautiful summer night, when all nature seemed hushed in ecstasy, the last blush gone that told of the sun's parting, Monsieur Vignevielle, in the course of one of those contemplative, uncompanioned walks which it was his habit to take, came slowly along the more open portion of the Rue Royale, with a step which was soft without intention, occasionally touching the end of his stout cane gently to the ground and looking upward among his old acquaintances, the stars.

It was one of those southern nights under whose spell all the sterner energies of the mind cloak themselves and lie down in bivouac, and the fancy and the imagination, that cannot sleep, slip their fetters and escape, beckoned away from behind every flowering bush and sweet-smelling tree, and every stretch of lonely, half-lighted walk, by the genius of poetry. The air stirred softly now and then, and was still again, as if the breezes lifted their expectant pinions and lowered them once more, awaiting the rising of the moon in a silence which fell upon the fields, the roads, the gardens, the walls, and the suburban and half-suburban streets, like a pause in worship. And anon she rose.

Monsieur Vignevielle's steps were bent toward the more central part of the town, and he was presently passing along a high, close, board-fence, on the right-hand side of the way, when, just within this inclosure, and almost overhead, in the dark boughs of a large orange-tree, a mocking-bird began the first low flute-notes of his all-night song. It may have been only the nearness of the songster that attracted the passer's attention, but he paused and looked up.

And then he remarked something more,—that the air where he had stopped was filled with the overpowering sweetness of the night-jasmine. He looked around; it could only be inside the fence. There was a gate just there. Would he push it, as his wont was? The grass was growing about it in a thick turf, as though the entrance had not been used for years. An iron staple clasped the cross-bar, and was driven deep into the gate-post. But now an eye that had been in the blacksmithing business—an eye which had later received high training as an eye for fastenings—fell upon that staple, and saw at a glance that the wood had shrunk from it, and it had sprung from its hold, though without falling out. The strange habit asserted itself; he laid his large hand upon the cross-bar; the turf at the base yielded, and the tall gate was drawn partly open.

At that moment, as at the moment whenever he drew or pushed a door or gate, or looked in at a window, he was thinking of one, the image of whose face and form had never left his inner vision since the day it had met him in his life's path and turned him face about from the way of destruction.

The bird ceased. The cause of the interruption, standing within the opening, saw before him, much obscured by its own numerous shadows, a broad, ill-kept, many-flowered garden, among whose untrimmed rose-trees and tangled vines, and often, also, in its old walks of pounded shell, the coco-grass and crab-grass had spread riotously, and sturdy weeds stood up in bloom. He stepped in and drew the gate to after him. There, very near by, was the clump of jasmine, whose ravishing odor had tempted him. It stood just beyond a brightly moonlit path, which turned from him in a curve toward the residence, a little distance to the right, and escaped the view at a point where it seemed more than likely a door of the house might open upon it. While he still looked, there fell upon his ear, from around that curve, a light footstep on the broken shells,—one only, and then all was for a moment still again. Had he mistaken? No. The same soft click was repeated nearer by, a pale glimpse of robes came through the tangle, and then, plainly to view, appeared an outline—a presence—a form—a spirit—a girl!

From throat to instep she was as white as Cynthia. Something above the medium height, slender, lithe, her abundant hair rolling in dark, rich waves back from her brows and down from her crown, and falling in two heavy plaits beyond her round, broadly girt waist and full to her knees, a few escaping locks eddying lightly on her graceful neck and her temples,—her arms, half hid in a snowy mist of sleeve, let down to guide her spotless skirts free from the dewy touch of the grass,—straight down the path she came!

Will she stop? Will she turn aside? Will she espy the dark form in the deep shade of the orange, and, with one piercing scream, wheel and vanish? She draws near. She approaches the jasmine; she raises her arms, the sleeves falling like a vapor down to the shoulders; rises upon tiptoe, and plucks a spray. O Memory! Can it be? *Can it be?* Is this his quest, or is it lunacy? The ground seems to M. Vignevielle the unsteady sea, and he to stand once more on a deck. And she? As she is now, if she but turn toward the orange, the whole glory of the moon will shine upon her face. His heart stands still; he is waiting for her to do that. She reaches up again; this time a bunch for her mother. That neck and throat! Now she fastens a spray in her hair. The mocking-bird cannot withhold; he breaks into song—she turns—she turns her face—it is she, it is she! Madame Delphine's daughter is the girl he met on the ship.

CHAPTER IX.
OLIVE.

She was just passing seventeen—that beautiful year when the heart of the maiden still beats quickly with the surprise of her new dominion, while with gentle dignity her brow accepts the holy coronation of womanhood. The forehead and temples beneath her loosely bound hair were fair without paleness, and meek without languor. She had the soft, lacklustre beauty of the South; no ruddiness of coral, no waxen white, no pink of shell; no heavenly blue in the glance; but a face that seemed, in all its other beauties, only a tender accompaniment for the large, brown, melting eyes, where the openness of child-nature mingled dreamily with the sweet mysteries of maiden thought. We say no color of shell on face or throat; but this was no deficiency, that which took its place being the warm, transparent tint of sculptured ivory.

This side door-way which led from Madame Delphine's house into her garden was overarched partly by an old remnant of vine-covered lattice, and partly by a crape-myrtle, against whose small, polished trunk leaned a rustic seat. Here Madame Delphine and Olive loved to sit when the twilights were balmy or the moon was bright.

"*Chérie*," said Madame Delphine on one of these evenings, "why do you dream so much?"

She spoke in the *patois* most natural to her, and which her daughter had easily learned.

The girl turned her face to her mother, and smiled, then dropped her glance to the hands in her own lap, which were listlessly handling the end of a ribbon. The mother looked at her with fond solicitude. Her dress was white again; this was but one night since that in which Monsieur Vignevielle had seen her at the bush of night-jasmine. He had not been discovered, but had gone away, shutting the gate, and leaving it as he had found it.

Her head was uncovered. Its plaited masses, quite black in the moonlight, hung down and coiled upon the bench, by her side. Her chaste drapery was of that revived classic order which the world of fashion was again laying aside to re-assume the mediæval bondage of the stay-lace; for New Orleans was behind the fashionable world, and Madame Delphine and her daughter were behind New Orleans. A delicate scarf, pale blue, of lightly netted worsted, fell from either shoulder down beside her hands. The look that was bent upon her changed perforce to one of gentle admiration. She seemed the goddess of the garden.

Olive glanced up. Madame Delphine was not prepared for the movement, and on that account repeated her question:

"What are you thinking about?"

The dreamer took the hand that was laid upon hers between her own palms, bowed her head, and gave them a soft kiss.

The mother submitted. Wherefore, in the silence which followed, a daughter's conscience felt the burden of having withheld an answer, and Olive presently said, as the pair sat looking up into the sky:

"I was thinking of Père Jerome's sermon."

Madame Delphine had feared so. Olive had lived on it ever since the day it was preached. The poor mother was almost ready to repent having ever afforded her the opportunity of hearing it. Meat and drink had become of secondary value to her daughter; she fed upon the sermon.

Olive felt her mother's thought and knew that her mother knew her own; but now that she had confessed, she would ask a question:

"Do you think, *maman*, that Père Jerome knows it was I who gave that missal?"

"No," said Madame Delphine, "I am sure he does not."

Another question came more timidly:

"Do—do you think he knows *him*?"

"Yes, I do. He said in his sermon he did."

Both remained for a long time very still, watching the moon gliding in and through among the small dark-and-white clouds. At last the daughter spoke again.

"I wish I was Père—I wish I was as good as Père Jerome."

"My child," said Madame Delphine, her tone betraying a painful summoning of strength to say what she had lacked the courage to utter,—"my child, I pray the good God you will not let your heart go after one whom you may never see in this world!"

The maiden turned her glance, and their eyes met. She cast her arms about her mother's neck, laid her cheek upon it for a moment, and then, feeling the maternal tear, lifted her lips, and, kissing her, said:

"I will not! I will not!"

But the voice was one, not of willing consent, but of desperate resolution.

"It would be useless, anyhow," said the mother, laying her arm around her daughter's waist.

Olive repeated the kiss, prolonging it passionately.

"I have nobody but you," murmured the girl; "I am a poor quadroone!"

She threw back her plaited hair for a third embrace, when a sound in the shrubbery startled them.

"*Qui ci ça?*" called Madame Delphine, in a frightened voice, as the two stood up, holding to each other.

No answer.

"It was only the dropping of a twig," she whispered, after a long holding of the breath. But they went into the house and barred it everywhere.

It was no longer pleasant to sit up. They retired, and in course of time, but not soon, they fell asleep, holding each other very tight, and fearing, even in their dreams, to hear another twig fall.

CHAPTER X.
BIRDS.

Monsieur Vignevielle looked in at no more doors or windows; but if the disappearance of this symptom was a favorable sign, others came to notice which were especially bad,—for instance, wakefulness. At well-nigh any hour of the night, the city guard, which itself dared not patrol singly, would meet him on his slow, unmolested, sky-gazing walk.

"Seems to enjoy it," said Jean Thompson; "the worst sort of evidence. If he showed distress of mind, it would not be so bad; but his calmness,—ugly feature."

The attorney had held his ground so long that he began really to believe it was tenable.

By day, it is true, Monsieur Vignevielle was at his post in his quiet "bank." Yet here, day by day, he was the source of more and more vivid astonishment to those who held preconceived notions of a banker's calling. As a banker, at least, he was certainly out of balance; while as a promenader, it seemed to those who watched him that his ruling idea had now veered about, and that of late he was ever on the quiet alert, not to find, but to evade, somebody.

"Olive, my child," whispered Madame Delphine one morning, as the pair were kneeling side by side on the tiled floor of the church, "yonder is Miché Vignevielle! If you will only look at once—he is just passing a little in———. Ah, much too slow again; he stepped out by the side door."

The mother thought it a strange providence that Monsieur Vignevielle should always be disappearing whenever Olive was with her.

One early dawn, Madame Delphine, with a small empty basket on her arm, stepped out upon the *banquette* in front of her house, shut and fastened the door very softly, and stole out in the direction whence you could faintly catch, in the stillness of the daybreak, the songs of the Gascon butchers and the pounding of their meat-axes on the stalls of the distant market-house. She was going to see if she could find some birds for Olive,—the child's appetite was so poor; and, as she was out, she would drop an early prayer at the cathedral. Faith and works.

"One must venture something, sometimes, in the cause of religion," thought she, as she started timorously on her way. But she had not gone a dozen steps before she repented her temerity. There was some one behind her.

33

There should not be anything terrible in a footstep merely because it is masculine; but Madame Delphine's mind was not prepared to consider that. A terrible secret was haunting her. Yesterday morning she had found a shoe-track in the garden. She had not disclosed the discovery to Olive, but she had hardly closed her eyes the whole night.

The step behind her now might be the fall of that very shoe. She quickened her pace, but did not leave the sound behind. She hurried forward almost at a run; yet it was still there—no farther, no nearer. Two frights were upon her at once—one for herself, another for Olive, left alone in the house; but she had but the one prayer—"God protect my child!" After a fearful time she reached a place of safety, the cathedral. There, panting, she knelt long enough to know the pursuit was, at least, suspended, and then arose, hoping and praying all the saints that she might find the way clear for her return in all haste to Olive.

She approached a different door from that by which she had entered, her eyes in all directions and her heart in her throat.

"Madame Carraze."

She started wildly and almost screamed, though the voice was soft and mild. Monsieur Vignevielle came slowly forward from the shade of the wall. They met beside a bench, upon which she dropped her basket.

"Ah, Miché Vignevielle, I thang de good God to mid you!"

"Is dad so, Madame Carraze? Fo' w'y dad is?"

"A man was chase me all dad way since my 'ouse!"

"Yes, Madame, I sawed him."

"You sawed 'im? Oo it was?"

"'Twas only one man wad is a foolizh. De people say he's crezzie. *Mais*, he don' goin' to meg you no 'arm."

"But I was scare' fo' my lill' girl."

"Noboddie don' goin' trouble you' lill' gal, Madame Carraze."

Madame Delphine looked up into the speaker's strangely kind and patient eyes, and drew sweet re-assurance from them.

"Madame," said Monsieur Vignevielle, "wad pud you hout so hearly dis morning?"

She told him her errand. She asked if he thought she would find anything.

"Yez," he said, "it was possible—a few lill' *bécassines-de-mer*, ou somezin' ligue. But fo' w'y you lill' gal lose doze hapetide?"

"Ah, Miché,"—Madame Delphine might have tried a thousand times again without ever succeeding half so well in lifting the curtain upon the whole, sweet, tender, old, old-fashioned truth,— "Ah, Miché, she wone tell me!"

"Bud, anny'ow, Madame, wad you thing?"

"Miché," she replied, looking up again with a tear standing in either eye, and then looking down once more as she began to speak, "I thing—I thing she's lonesome."

"You thing?"

She nodded.

"Ah! Madame Carraze," he said, partly extending his hand, "you see? 'Tis impossible to mague you' owze shud so tighd to priv-en dad. Madame, I med one mizteg."

"Ah, *non*, Miché!"

"Yez. There har nod one poss'bil'ty fo' me to be dad guardian of you' daughteh!"

Madame Delphine started with surprise and alarm.

"There is ondly one wad can be," he continued.

"But oo, Miché?"

"God."

"Ah, Miché Vignevielle——" She looked at him appealingly.

"I don' goin' to dizzerd you, Madame Carraze," he said.

She lifted her eyes. They filled. She shook her head, a tear fell, she bit her lip, smiled, and suddenly dropped her face into both hands, sat down upon the bench and wept until she shook.

"You dunno wad I mean, Madame Carraze?"

She did not know.

"I mean dad guardian of you' daughteh godd to fine 'er now one 'uzban'; an' noboddie are hable to do dad egceb de good God 'imsev. But, Madame, I tell you wad I do."

She rose up. He continued:

"Go h-open you' owze; I fin' you' daughteh dad' uzban'."

Madame Delphine was a helpless, timid thing; but her eyes showed she was about to resent this offer. Monsieur Vignevielle put forth his hand—it touched her shoulder—and said, kindly still, and without eagerness.

35

"One w'ite man, Madame; 'tis prattycabble. I *know* 'tis prattycabble. One w'ite jantleman, Madame. You can truz me. I goin' fedge 'im. H-ondly you go h-open you' owze."

Madame Delphine looked down, twining her handkerchief among her fingers.

He repeated his proposition.

"You will come firz by you'se'f?" she asked.

"Iv you wand."

She lifted up once more her eye of faith. That was her answer.

"Come," he said, gently, "I wan' sen' some bird ad you' lill' gal."

And they went away, Madame Delphine's spirit grown so exaltedly bold that she said as they went, though a violent blush followed her words:

"Miché Vignevielle, I thing Père Jerome mighd be ab'e to tell you someboddie."

CHAPTER XI.
FACE TO FACE.

Madame Delphine found her house neither burned nor rifled.

"*Ah! ma piti sans popa*! Ah! my little fatherless one!" Her faded bonnet fell back between her shoulders, hanging on by the strings, and her dropped basket, with its "few lill' *bécassines-de-mer*" dangling from the handle, rolled out its okra and soup-joint upon the floor. "*Ma piti*! kiss!—kiss!—kiss!"

"But is it good news you have, or bad?" cried the girl, a fourth or fifth time.

"*Dieu sait, ma c'ère; mo pas conné!*"—God knows, my darling; I cannot tell!

The mother dropped into a chair, covered her face with her apron, and burst into tears, then looked up with an effort to smile, and wept afresh.

"What have you been doing?" asked the daughter, in a long-drawn, fondling tone. She leaned forward and unfastened her mother's bonnet-strings. "Why do you cry?"

"For nothing at all, my darling; for nothing—I am such a fool."

The girl's eyes filled. The mother looked up into her face and said:

"No, it is nothing, nothing, only that—" turning her head from side to side with a slow, emotional emphasis, "Miché Vignevielle is the best—*best* man on the good Lord's earth!"

Olive drew a chair close to her mother, sat down and took the little yellow hands into her own white lap, and looked tenderly into her eyes. Madame Delphine felt herself yielding; she must make a show of telling something:

"He sent you those birds!"

The girl drew her face back a little. The little woman turned away, trying in vain to hide her tearful smile, and they laughed together, Olive mingling a daughter's fond kiss with her laughter.

"There is something else," she said, "and you shall tell me."

"Yes," replied Madame Delphine, "only let me get composed."

But she did not get so. Later in the morning she came to Olive with the timid yet startling proposal that they would do what they could to brighten up the long-neglected front room. Olive was mystified and troubled, but consented, and thereupon the mother's spirits rose.

The work began, and presently ensued all the thumping, the trundling, the lifting and letting down, the raising and swallowing of dust, and the smells of turpentine, brass, pumice and woollen rags that go to characterize a housekeeper's *émeute*; and still, as the work progressed, Madame Delphine's heart grew light, and her little black eyes sparkled.

"We like a clean parlor, my daughter, even though no one is ever coming to see us, eh?" she said, as entering the apartment she at last sat down, late in the afternoon. She had put on her best attire.

Olive was not there to reply. The mother called but got no answer. She rose with an uneasy heart, and met her a few steps beyond the door that opened into the garden, in a path which came up from an old latticed bower. Olive was approaching slowly, her face pale and wild. There was an agony of hostile dismay in the look, and the trembling and appealing tone with which, taking the frightened mother's cheeks between her palms, she said:

"*Ah! ma mère, qui vini 'ci ce soir?*"—Who is coming here this evening?

"Why, my dear child, I was just saying, we like a clean——"

But the daughter was desperate:

"Oh, tell me, my mother, *who* is coming?"

"My darling, it is our blessed friend, Miché Vignevielle!"

"To see me?" cried the girl.

"Yes."

"Oh, my mother, what have you done?"

"Why, Olive, my child," exclaimed the little mother, bursting into tears, "do you forget it is Miché Vignevielle who has promised to protect you when I die?"

The daughter had turned away, and entered the door; but she faced around again, and extending her arms toward her mother, cried:

"How can—he is a white man—I am a poor——"

"Ah! *chérie*" replied Madame Delphine, seizing the outstretched hands, "it is there—it is there that he shows himself the best man alive! He sees that difficulty; he proposes to meet it; he says he will find you a suitor!"

Olive freed her hands violently, motioned her mother back, and stood proudly drawn up, flashing an indignation too great for speech; but the next moment she had uttered a cry, and was sobbing on the floor.

The mother knelt beside her and threw an arm about her shoulders.

"Oh, my sweet daughter, you must not cry! I did not want to tell you at all! I did not want to tell you! It isn't fair for you to cry so hard. Miché Vignevielle says you shall have the one you wish, or none at all, Olive, or none at all."

"None at all! none at all! None, none, none!"

"No, no, Olive," said the mother, "none at all. He brings none with him to-night, and shall bring none with him hereafter."

Olive rose suddenly, silently declined her mother's aid, and went alone to their chamber in the half-story.

Madame Delphine wandered drearily from door to window, from window to door, and presently into the newly-furnished front room which now seemed dismal beyond degree. There was a great Argand lamp in one corner. How she had labored that day to prepare it for evening illumination! A little beyond it, on the wall, hung a crucifix. She knelt under it, with her eyes fixed upon it, and thus silently remained until its outline was undistinguishable in the deepening shadows of evening.

She arose. A few minutes later, as she was trying to light the lamp, an approaching step on the sidewalk seemed to pause. Her heart stood still. She softly laid the phosphorus-box out of her hands. A shoe grated softly on the stone step, and Madame Delphine, her heart beating in great thuds, without waiting for a knock, opened the door, bowed low, and exclaimed in a soft perturbed voice:

"Miché Vignevielle!"

He entered, hat in hand, and with that almost noiseless tread which we have noticed. She gave him a chair and closed the door; then hastened, with words of apology, back to her task of lighting the lamp. But her hands paused in their work again,—Olive's step was on the stairs; then it came off the stairs; then it was in the next room, and then there was the whisper of soft robes, a breath of gentle perfume, and a snowy figure in the door. She was dressed for the evening.

"Maman?"

Madame Delphine was struggling desperately with the lamp, and at that moment it responded with a tiny bead of light.

"I am here, my daughter."

She hastened to the door, and Olive, all unaware of a third presence, lifted her white arms, laid them about her mother's neck, and, ignoring her effort to speak, wrested a fervent kiss from her lips. The crystal of the lamp sent out a faint gleam; it grew; it spread on every side; the ceiling, the walls lighted up; the crucifix, the furniture of the room came back into shape.

"Maman!" cried Olive, with a tremor of consternation.

"It is Miché Vignevielle, my daughter——"

The gloom melted swiftly away before the eyes of the startled maiden, a dark form stood out against the farther wall, and the light, expanding to the full, shone clearly upon the unmoving figure and quiet face of Capitaine Lemaitre.

CHAPTER XII.
THE MOTHER BIRD.

One afternoon, some three weeks after Capitaine Lemaitre had called on Madame Delphine, the priest started to make a pastoral call and had hardly left the gate of his cottage, when a person, overtaking him, plucked his gown:

"Père Jerome——"

He turned.

The face that met his was so changed with excitement and distress that for an instant he did not recognize it.

"Why, Madame Delphine——"

"Oh, Père Jerome! I wan' see you so bad, so bad! *Mo oulé dit quiç'ose,*—I godd some' to tell you."

The two languages might be more successful than one, she seemed to think.

"We had better go back to my parlor," said the priest, in their native tongue.

They returned.

Madame Delphine's very step was altered,—nervous and inelastic. She swung one arm as she walked, and brandished a turkey-tail fan.

"I was glad, yass, to kedge you," she said, as they mounted the front, outdoor stair; following her speech with a slight, unmusical laugh, and fanning herself with unconscious fury.

"*Fé chaud,*" she remarked again, taking the chair he offered and continuing to ply the fan.

Père Jerome laid his hat upon a chest of drawers, sat down opposite her, and said, as he wiped his kindly face:

"Well, Madame Carraze?"

Gentle as the tone was, she started, ceased fanning, lowered the fan to her knee, and commenced smoothing its feathers.

"Père Jerome——" She gnawed her lip and shook her head.

"Well?"

She burst into tears.

The priest rose and loosed the curtain of one of the windows. He did it slowly—as slowly as he could, and, as he came back, she lifted her face with sudden energy, and exclaimed:

"Oh, Père Jerome, de law is brogue! de law is brogue! I brogue it! 'Twas me! 'Twas me!"

The tears gushed out again, but she shut her lips very tight, and dumbly turned away her face. Père Jerome waited a little before replying; then he said, very gently:

"I suppose dad muss 'ave been by accyden', Madame Delphine?"

The little father felt a wish—one which he often had when weeping women were before him—that he were an angel instead of a man, long enough to press the tearful cheek upon his breast, and assure the weeper God would not let the lawyers and judges hurt her. He allowed a few moments more to pass, and then asked:

"*N'est-ce-pas*, Madame Delphine? Daz ze way, aint it?"

"No, Père Jerome, no. My daughter—oh, Père Jerome, I bethroath my lill' girl—to a w'ite man!" And immediately Madame Delphine commenced savagely drawing a thread in the fabric of her skirt with one trembling hand, while she drove the fan with the other. "Dey goin' git marry."

On the priest's face came a look of pained surprise. He slowly said:

"Is dad possib', Madame Delphine?"

"Yass," she replied, at first without lifting her eyes; and then again, "Yass," looking full upon him through her tears, "yass, 'tis tru'."

He rose and walked once across the room, returned, and said, in the Creole dialect:

"Is he a good man—without doubt?"

"De bez in God's world!" replied Madame Delphine, with a rapturous smile.

"My poor, dear friend," said the priest, "I am afraid you are being deceived by somebody."

There was the pride of an unswerving faith in the triumphant tone and smile with which she replied, raising and slowly shaking her head:

"Ah-h, no-o-o, Miché! Ah-h, no, no! Not by Ursin Lemaitre-Vignevielle!"

Père Jerome was confounded. He turned again, and, with his hands at his back and his eyes cast down, slowly paced the floor.

"He *is* a good man," he said, by and by, as if he thought aloud. At length he halted before the woman.

"Madame Delphine——"

The distressed glance with which she had been following his steps was lifted to his eyes.

"Suppose dad should be true w'at doze peop' say 'bout Ursin."

"*Qui ci ça?* What is that?" asked the quadroone, stopping her fan.

"Some peop' say Ursin is crezzie."

41

"Ah, Père Jerome!" She leaped to her feet as if he had smitten her, and putting his words away with an outstretched arm and wide-open palm, suddenly lifted hands and eyes to heaven, and cried: "I wizh to God—*I wizh to God*—de whole worl' was crezzie dad same way!" She sank, trembling, into her chair. "Oh, no, no," she continued, shaking her head, "'tis not Miché Vignevielle w'at's crezzie." Her eyes lighted with sudden fierceness. "'Tis dad *law*! Dad *law* is crezzie! Dad law is a fool!"

A priest of less heart-wisdom might have replied that the law is—the law; but Père Jerome saw that Madame Delphine was expecting this very response. Wherefore he said, with gentleness:

"Madame Delphine, a priest is not a bailiff, but a physician. How can I help you?"

A grateful light shone a moment in her eyes, yet there remained a piteous hostility in the tone in which she demanded:

"*Mais, pou'quoi yé fé cette méchanique là?*"—What business had they to make that contraption?

His answer was a shrug with his palms extended and a short, disclamatory "Ah." He started to resume his walk, but turned to her again and said:

"Why did they make that law? Well, they made it to keep the two races separate."

Madame Delphine startled the speaker with a loud, harsh, angry laugh. Fire came from her eyes and her lip curled with scorn.

"Then they made a lie, Père Jerome! Separate! No-o-o! They do not want to keep us separated; no, no! But they *do* want to keep us despised!" She laid her hand on her heart, and frowned upward with physical pain. "But, very well! from which race do they want to keep my daughter separate? She is seven parts white! The law did not stop her from being that; and now, when she wants to be a white man's good and honest wife, shall that law stop her? Oh, no!" She rose up. "No; I will tell you what that law is made for. It is made to—punish—my—child—for—not—choosing—her—father! Père Jerome—my God, what a law!" She dropped back into her seat. The tears came in a flood, which she made no attempt to restrain.

"No," she began again—and here she broke into English—"fo' me I don' kyare; but, Père Jerome,—'tis fo' dat I come to tell you,—dey *shall not* punizh my daughter!" She was on her feet again, smiting her heaving bosom with the fan. "She shall marrie oo she want!"

Père Jerome had heard her out, not interrupting by so much as a motion of the hand. Now his decision was made, and he touched her softly with the ends of his fingers.

"Madame Delphine, I want you to go at 'ome. Go at 'ome."

"Wad you goin' mague?" she asked.

"Nottin'. But go at 'ome. Kip quite; don' put you'se'f sig. I goin' see Ursin. We trah to figs dat law fo' you."

"You kin figs dad!" she cried, with a gleam of joy.

"We goin' to try, Madame Delphine. Adieu!"

He offered his hand. She seized and kissed it thrice, covering it with tears, at the same time lifting up her eyes to his and murmuring:

"De bez man God evva mague!"

At the door she turned to offer a more conventional good-bye; but he was following her out, bareheaded. At the gate they paused an instant, and then parted with a simple adieu, she going home and he returning for his hat, and starting again upon his interrupted business.

Before he came back to his own house, he stopped at the lodgings of Monsieur Vignevielle, but did not find him in.

"Indeed," the servant at the door said, "he said he might not return for some days or weeks."

So Père Jerome, much wondering, made a second detour toward the residence of one of Monsieur Vignevielle's employés.

"Yes," said the clerk, "his instructions are to hold the business, as far as practicable, in suspense, during his absence. Everything is in another name." And then he whispered:

"Officers of the Government looking for him. Information got from some of the prisoners taken months ago by the United States brig *Porpoise*. But"—a still softer whisper—"have no fear; they will never find him: Jean Thompson and Evariste Varrillat have hid him away too well for that."

CHAPTER XIII.
TRIBULATION.

The Saturday following was a very beautiful day. In the morning a light fall of rain had passed across the town, and all the afternoon you could see signs, here and there upon the horizon, of other showers. The ground was dry again, while the breeze was cool and sweet, smelling of wet foliage and bringing sunshine and shade in frequent and very pleasing alternation.

There was a walk in Père Jerome's little garden, of which we have not spoken, off on the right side of the cottage, with his chamber window at one end, a few old and twisted, but blossom-laden, crape-myrtles on either hand, now and then a rose of some unpretending variety and some bunches of rue, and at the other end a shrine, in whose blue niche stood a small figure of Mary, with folded hands and uplifted eyes. No other window looked down upon the spot, and its seclusion was often a great comfort to Père Jerome.

Up and down this path, but a few steps in its entire length, the priest was walking, taking the air for a few moments after a prolonged sitting in the confessional. Penitents had been numerous this afternoon. He was thinking of Ursin. The officers of the Government had not found him, nor had Père Jerome seen him; yet he believed they had, in a certain indirect way, devised a simple project by which they could at any time "figs dad law," providing only that these Government officials would give over their search; for, though he had not seen the fugitive, Madame Delphine had seen him, and had been the vehicle of communication between them. There was an orange-tree, where a mocking-bird was wont to sing and a girl in white to walk, that the detectives wot not of. The law was to be "figs" by the departure of the three frequenters of the jasmine-scented garden in one ship to France, where the law offered no obstacles.

It seemed moderately certain to those in search of Monsieur Vignevielle (and it was true) that Jean and Evariste were his harborers; but for all that the hunt, even for clues, was vain. The little banking establishment had not been disturbed. Jean Thompson had told the searchers certain facts about it, and about its gentle proprietor as well, that persuaded them to make no move against the concern, if the same relations did not even induce a relaxation of their efforts for his personal discovery.

Père Jerome was walking to and fro, with his hands behind him, pondering these matters. He had paused a moment at the end of the walk furthest from his window, and was looking around upon the sky, when, turning, he beheld a closely veiled female figure standing at the other end, and knew instantly that it was Olive.

She came forward quickly and with evident eagerness.

"I came to confession," she said, breathing hurriedly, the excitement in her eyes shining through her veil, "but I find I am too late."

"There is no too late or too early for that; I am always ready," said the priest. "But how is your mother?"

"Ah!——"

Her voice failed.

"More trouble?"

"Ah, sir, I have *made* trouble. Oh, Père Jerome, I am bringing so much trouble upon my poor mother!"

Père Jerome moved slowly toward the house, with his eyes cast down, the veiled girl at his side.

"It is not your fault," he presently said. And after another pause: "I thought it was all arranged."

He looked up and could see, even through the veil, her crimson blush.

"Oh, no," she replied, in a low, despairing voice, dropping her face.

"What is the difficulty?" asked the priest, stopping in the angle of the path, where it turned toward the front of the house.

She averted her face, and began picking the thin scales of bark from a crape-myrtle.

"Madame Thompson and her husband were at our house this morning. *He* had told Monsieur Thompson all about it. They were very kind to me at first, but they tried——" She was weeping.

"What did they try to do?" asked the priest.

"They tried to make me believe he is insane."

She succeeded in passing her handkerchief up under her veil.

"And I suppose then your poor mother grew angry, eh?"

"Yes; and they became much more so, and said if we did not write, or send a writing, to *him*, within twenty-four hours, breaking the——"

"Engagement," said Père Jerome.

45

"They would give him up to the Government. Oh, Père Jerome, what shall I do? It is killing my mother!"

She bowed her head and sobbed.

"Where is your mother now?"

"She has gone to see Monsieur Jean Thompson. She says she has a plan that will match them all. I do not know what it is. I begged her not to go; but oh, sir, *she is* crazy,—and—I am no better."

"My poor child," said Père Jerome, "what you seem to want is not absolution, but relief from persecution."

"Oh, father, I have committed mortal sin,—I am guilty of pride and anger."

"Nevertheless," said the priest, starting toward his front gate, "we will put off your confession. Let it go until to-morrow morning; you will find me in my box just before mass; I will hear you then. My child, I know that in your heart, now, you begrudge the time it would take; and that is right. There are moments when we are not in place even on penitential knees. It is so with you now. We must find your mother. Go you at once to your house; if she is there, comfort her as best you can, and *keep her in, if possible*, until I come. If she is not there, stay; leave me to find her; one of you, at least, must be where I can get word to you promptly. God comfort and uphold you. I hope you may find her at home; tell her, for me, not to fear,"—he lifted the gate-latch,—"that she and her daughter are of more value than many sparrows; that God's priest sends her that word from Him. Tell her to fix her trust in the great Husband of the Church, and she shall yet see her child receiving the grace-giving sacrament of matrimony. Go; I shall, in a few minutes, be on my way to Jean Thompson's, and shall find her, either there or wherever she is. Go; they shall not oppress you. Adieu!"

A moment or two later he was in the street himself.

CHAPTER XIV.
BY AN OATH.

Père Jerome, pausing on a street-corner in the last hour of sunlight, had wiped his brow and taken his cane down from under his arm to start again, when somebody, coming noiselessly from he knew not where, asked, so suddenly as to startle him:

"*Miché, commin yé 'pellé la rie ici?*—how do they call this street here?"

It was by the bonnet and dress, disordered though they were, rather than by the haggard face which looked distractedly around, that he recognized the woman to whom he replied in her own *patois*:

"It is the Rue Burgundy. Where are you going, Madame Delphine?"

She almost leaped from the ground.

"Oh, Père Jerome! *mo pas conné,*—I dunno. You know w'ere's dad 'ouse of Michè Jean Tomkin? *Mo courri 'ci, mo courri là,—mo pas capale li trouvé.* I go (run) here—there—I cannot find it," she gesticulated.

"I am going there myself," said he; "but why do you want to see Jean Thompson, Madame Delphine?"

"I '*blige*' to see 'im!" she replied, jerking herself half around away, one foot planted forward with an air of excited preoccupation; "I god some' to tell 'im wad I '*blige*' to tell 'im!"

"Madame Delphine——"

"Oh! Père Jerome, fo' de love of de good God, show me dad way to de 'ouse of Jean Tomkin!"

Her distressed smile implored pardon for her rudeness.

"What are you going to tell him?" asked the priest.

"Oh, Père Jerome,"—in the Creole *patois* again,—"I am going to put an end to all this trouble—only I pray you do not ask me about it now; every minute is precious!"

He could not withstand her look of entreaty.

"Come," he said, and they went.

Jean Thompson and Doctor Varrillat lived opposite each other on the Bayou road, a little way beyond the town limits as then prescribed. Each had his large, white-columned, four-sided house among the magnolias,—his huge live-oak overshadowing either corner of the darkly shaded garden, his broad, brick walk leading down to the tall, brick-pillared gate, his square of bright, red pavement on the turf-covered sidewalk, and his railed platform spanning the draining-ditch, with a pair of green benches, one on each edge, facing each other crosswise of the gutter. There, any sunset hour, you were sure to find the householder sitting beside his cool-robed matron, two or three slave nurses in white turbans standing at hand, and an excited throng of fair children, nearly all of a size.

Sometimes, at a beckon or call, the parents on one side of the way would join those on the other, and the children and nurses of both families would be given the liberty of the opposite platform and an ice-cream fund! Generally the parents chose the Thompson platform, its outlook being more toward the sunset.

Such happened to be the arrangement this afternoon. The two husbands sat on one bench and their wives on the other, both pairs very quiet, waiting respectfully for the day to die, and exchanging only occasional comments on matters of light moment as they passed through the memory. During one term of silence Madame Varrillat, a pale, thin-faced, but cheerful-looking lady, touched Madame Thompson, a person of two and a half times her weight, on her extensive and snowy bare elbow, directing her attention obliquely up and across the road.

About a hundred yards distant, in the direction of the river, was a long, pleasantly shaded green strip of turf, destined in time for a sidewalk. It had a deep ditch on the nearer side, and a fence of rough cypress palisades on the farther, and these were overhung, on the one hand, by a row of bitter orange-trees inside the inclosure, and, on the other, by a line of slanting china-trees along the outer edge of the ditch. Down this cool avenue two figures were approaching side by side. They had first attracted Madame Varrillat's notice by the bright play of sunbeams which, as they walked, fell upon them in soft, golden flashes through the chinks between the palisades.

Madame Thompson elevated a pair of glasses which were no detraction from her very good looks, and remarked, with the serenity of a reconnoitering general:

"*Père Jerome et cette milatraise.*"

All eyes were bent toward them.

"She walks like a man," said Madame Varrillat, in the language with which the conversation had opened.

"No," said the physician, "like a woman in a state of high nervous excitement."

Jean Thompson kept his eyes on the woman, and said:

"She must not forget to walk like a woman in the State of Louisiana,"—as near as the pun can be translated. The company laughed. Jean Thompson looked at his wife, whose applause he prized, and she answered by an asseverative toss of the head, leaning back and contriving, with some effort, to get her arms folded. Her laugh was musical and low, but enough to make the folded arms shake gently up and down.

"Père Jerome is talking to her," said one. The priest was at that moment endeavoring, in the interest of peace, to say a good word for the four people who sat watching his approach. It was in the old strain:

"Blame them one part, Madame Delphine, and their fathers, mothers, brothers, and fellow-citizens the other ninety-nine."

But to everything she had the one amiable answer which Père Jerome ignored:

"I am going to arrange it to satisfy everybody, all together. *Tout à fait.*"

"They are coming here," said Madame Varrillat, half articulately.

"Well, of course," murmured another; and the four rose up, smiling courteously, the doctor and attorney advancing and shaking hands with the priest.

No—Père Jerome thanked them—he could not sit down.

"This, I believe you know, Jean, is Madame Delphine——"
The quadroone curtsied.

"A friend of mine," he added, smiling kindly upon her, and turning, with something imperative in his eye, to the group. "She says she has an important private matter to communicate."

"To me?" asked Jean Thompson.

"To all of you; so I will—— Good-evening." He responded nothing to the expressions of regret, but turned to Madame Delphine. She murmured something.

"Ah! yes, certainly." He addressed the company: "She wishes me to speak for her veracity; it is unimpeachable. "Well, good-evening." He shook hands and departed.

The four resumed their seats, and turned their eyes upon the standing figure.

"Have you something to say to us?" asked Jean Thompson, frowning at her law-defying bonnet.

"*Oui,*" replied the woman, shrinking to one side, and laying hold of one of the benches, "*mo oulé di' tou' ç'ose*"—I want to tell everything. "*Miché Vignevielle la plis bon homme di moune*"—the best man in the world; "*mo pas capabe li fé tracas*"—I cannot give him trouble. "*Mo pas capabe, non; m'olé di' tous ç'ose.*" She attempted to fan herself, her face turned away from the attorney, and her eyes rested on the ground.

"Take a seat," said Doctor Varrillat, with some suddenness, starting from his place and gently guiding her sinking form into the corner of the bench. The ladies rose up; somebody had to stand; the two races could not both sit down at once—at least not in that public manner.

"Your salts," said the physician to his wife. She handed the vial. Madame Delphine stood up again.

"We will all go inside," said Madame Thompson, and they passed through the gate and up the walk, mounted the steps, and entered the deep, cool drawing-room.

Madame Thompson herself bade the quadroone be seated.

"Well?" said Jean Thompson, as the rest took chairs.

"*C'est drole*"—it's funny—said Madame Delphine, with a piteous effort to smile, "that nobody thought of it. It is so plain. You have only to look and see. I mean about Olive." She loosed a button in the front of her dress and passed her hand into her bosom. "And yet, Olive herself never thought of it. She does not know a word."

The hand came out holding a miniature. Madame Varrillat passed it to Jean Thompson.

"*Ouala so popa*" said Madame Delphine. "That is her father."

It went from one to another, exciting admiration and murmured praise.

"She is the image of him," said Madame Thompson, in an austere under-tone, returning it to her husband.

Doctor Varrillat was watching Madame Delphine. She was very pale. She had passed a trembling hand into a pocket of her skirt, and now drew out another picture, in a case the counterpart of the first. He reached out for it, and she handed it to him. He looked at it a moment, when his eyes suddenly lighted up and he passed it to the attorney.

"*Et là*"—Madame Delphine's utterance failed—"*et là, ouala sa moman.*" (That is her mother.)

The three others instantly gathered around Jean Thompson's chair. They were much impressed.

"It is true beyond a doubt!" muttered Madame Thompson.

Madame Varrillat looked at her with astonishment.

"The proof is right there in the faces," said Madame Thompson.

"Yes! yes!" said Madame Delphine, excitedly; "the proof is there! You do not want any better! I am willing to swear to it! But you want no better proof! That is all anybody could want! My God! you cannot help but see it!"

Her manner was wild.

Jean Thompson looked at her sternly.

"Nevertheless you say you are willing to take your solemn oath to this."

"Certainly——"

"You will have to do it."

"Certainly, Miché Thompson, *of course* I shall; you will make out the paper and I will swear before God that it is true! Only"—turning to the ladies—"do not tell Olive; she will never believe it. It will break her heart! It——"

A servant came and spoke privately to Madame Thompson, who rose quickly and went to the hall. Madame Delphine continued, rising unconsciously:

"You see, I have had her with me from a baby. She knows no better. He brought her to me only two months old. Her mother had died in the ship, coming out here. He did not come straight from home here. His people never knew he was married!"

The speaker looked around suddenly with a startled glance. There was a noise of excited speaking in the hall.

"It is not true, Madame Thompson!" cried a girl's voice.

Madame Delphine's look became one of wildest distress and alarm, and she opened her lips in a vain attempt to utter some request, when Olive appeared a moment in the door, and then flew into her arms.

"My mother! my mother! my mother!"

Madame Thompson, with tears in her eyes, tenderly drew them apart and let Madame Delphine down into her chair, while Olive threw herself upon her knees, continuing to cry:

"Oh, my mother! Say you are my mother!"

Madame Delphine looked an instant into the upturned face, and then turned her own away, with a long, low cry of pain, looked again, and laying both hands upon the suppliant's head, said:

"*Oh, chère piti à moin, to pa' ma fie!*" (Oh, my darling little one, you are not my daughter!) Her eyes closed, and her head sank back; the two gentlemen sprang to her assistance, and laid her upon a sofa unconscious.

When they brought her to herself, Olive was kneeling at her head silently weeping.

"*Maman, chère maman!*" said the girl softly, kissing her lips.

"*Ma courri c'ez moin*" (I will go home), said the mother, drearily.

"You will go home with me," said Madame Varrillat, with great kindness of manner—"just across the street here; I will take care of you till you feel better. And Olive will stay here with Madame Thompson. You will be only the width of the street apart."

But Madame Delphine would go nowhere but to her home. Olive she would not allow to go with her. Then they wanted to send a servant or two to sleep in the house with her for aid and protection; but all she would accept was the transient service of a messenger to invite two of her kinspeople—man and wife—to come and make their dwelling with her.

In course of time these two—a poor, timid, helpless, pair—fell heir to the premises. Their children had it after them; but, whether in those hands or these, the house had its habits and continued in them; and to this day the neighbors, as has already been said, rightly explain its close-sealed, uninhabited look by the all-sufficient statement that the inmates "is quadroons."

CHAPTER XV.
KYRIE ELEISON.

The second Saturday afternoon following was hot and calm. The lamp burning before the tabernacle in Père Jerome's little church might have hung with as motionless a flame in the window behind. The lilies of St. Joseph's wand, shining in one of the half opened panes, were not more completely at rest than the leaves on tree and vine without, suspended in the slumbering air. Almost as still, down under the organ-gallery, with a single band of light falling athwart his box from a small door which stood ajar, sat the little priest, behind the lattice of the confessional, silently wiping away the sweat that beaded on his brow and rolled down his face. At distant intervals the shadow of some one entering softly through the door would obscure, for a moment, the band of light, and an aged crone, or a little boy, or some gentle presence that the listening confessor had known only by the voice for many years, would kneel a few moments beside his waiting ear, in prayer for blessing and in review of those slips and errors which prove us all akin.

The day had been long and fatiguing. First, early mass; a hasty meal; then a business call upon the archbishop in the interest of some projected charity; then back to his cottage, and so to the banking-house of "Vignevielle," in the Rue Toulouse. There all was open, bright, and re-assured, its master virtually, though not actually, present. The search was over and the seekers gone, personally wiser than they would tell, and officially reporting that (to the best of their knowledge and belief, based on evidence, and especially on the assurances of an unexceptionable eyewitness, to wit, Monsieur Vignevielle, banker) Capitaine Lemaitre was dead and buried. At noon there had been a wedding in the little church. Its scenes lingered before Père Jerome's vision now—the kneeling pair: the bridegroom, rich in all the excellences of man, strength and kindness slumbering interlocked in every part and feature; the bride, a saintly weariness on her pale face, her awesome eyes lifted in adoration upon the image of the Saviour; the small knots of friends behind: Madame Thompson, large, fair, self-contained; Jean Thompson, with the affidavit of Madame Delphine showing through his tightly buttoned coat; the physician and his wife, sharing one expression of amiable consent; and last—yet first— one small, shrinking female figure, here at one side, in faded robes and dingy bonnet. She sat as motionless as stone, yet wore a look of apprehension, and in the small, restless black eyes which peered out from the pinched and wasted face, betrayed the peacelessness of a harrowed mind; and neither the recollection of bride, nor of groom, nor of potential friends behind, nor the occupation of the present hour, could shut out from the tired priest the image of that woman, or the sound of his own low words of invitation to her, given as the company left the church—"Come to confession this afternoon."

By and by a long time passed without the approach of any step, or any glancing of light or shadow, save for the occasional progress from station to station of some one over on the right who was noiselessly going the way of the cross. Yet Père Jerome tarried.

"She will surely come," he said to himself; "she promised she would come."

A moment later, his sense, quickened by the prolonged silence, caught a subtle evidence or two of approach, and the next moment a penitent knelt noiselessly at the window of his box, and the whisper came tremblingly, in the voice he had waited to hear:

"*Bénissez-moin, mo' Père, pa'ce que mo péché.*" (Bless me, father, for I have sinned.)

He gave his blessing.

"*Ainsi soit-il*—Amen," murmured the penitent, and then, in the soft accents of the Creole *patois*, continued:

"'I confess to Almighty God, to the blessed Mary, ever Virgin, to blessed Michael the Archangel, to blessed John the Baptist, to the holy Apostles Peter and Paul, and to all the saints, that I have sinned exceedingly in thought, word, and deed, *through my fault, through my fault, through my most grievous fault.*' I confessed on Saturday, three weeks ago, and received absolution, and I have performed the penance enjoined. Since then——" There she stopped.

There was a soft stir, as if she sank slowly down, and another as if she rose up again, and in a moment she said:

"Olive *is* my child. The picture I showed to Jean Thompson is the half-sister of my daughter's father, dead before my child was born. She is the image of her and of him; but, O God! Thou knowest! Oh Olive, my own daughter!"

She ceased, and was still. Père Jerome waited, but no sound came. He looked through the window. She was kneeling, with her forehead resting on her arms—motionless.

He repeated the words of absolution. Still she did not stir.

"My daughter," he said, "go to thy home in peace." But she did not move.

He rose hastily, stepped from the box, raised her in his arms, and called her by name:

"Madame Delphine!" Her head fell back in his elbow; for an instant there was life in the eyes—it glimmered—it vanished, and tears gushed from his own and fell upon the gentle face of the dead, as he looked up to heaven and cried:

"Lord, lay not this sin to her charge!"

12076363R00033

Made in the USA
San Bernardino, CA
06 June 2014